Twisters

Kathleen Ryder

DEDICATION

For Jenny, who likes a good twist in her stories.

TABLE OF CONTENTS

GOING DOWN 1

THE WEDDING 5

THE CLAIRVOYANT 9

THE GRAVE 13

SECRETS 17

THE COMPETITION 21

PRISON 25

THE CLEANER 29

THE LIBRARY 33

SEVEN DAYS 36

GOING DOWN

Alice watches the numbers above the elevator change slowly, a soft sigh escaping her lips. Perhaps she should have opted to take the stairs after all, if only she had worn her sensible shoes instead of these ridiculous ankle breaking ten-inch heels, she might have been halfway to the train station by now, and her comforting little home.

How she longed to climb into a warm bath and soak away the disappointment of the day. She had been so sure about this job and was absolutely certain that the interview was going well, that is, until it was interrupted. There was zero chance of working here now, not with the current owner dead in any case.

Right in the middle of explaining her experience with accounting software, the door had exploded furiously inwards, revealing the silhouette of a man with a gun in his hand. Before anyone could react, he had fired, her interviewer slumping in his chair, blood fanning out across his starched white shirt.

Seriously, Alice shook her head in disbelief, and wondered briefly if she would appear on the evening news. That would be something! A ding heralded the elevators arrival and Alice stepped inside, grateful to find only one other occupant. Alice pressed the button for the ground floor and leant back against the wall, studying the man opposite her.

"I know you," Alice smiled, recognition flaring in her eyes. "You're the man from the train yesterday, and the café this morning. It seems we keep running into each other lately, perhaps it is serendipity?"

"Perhaps it is," the man's lips twitched momentarily. "I'm Caleb, if I'm not mistaken you were heading to a job interview, how did that pan out?"

"Not so well actually, but I have another one tomorrow so fingers crossed," Alice answered, her usually upbeat voice sounding flat even to her own ears. She was exhausted, and starting to feel like death warmed up, she only hoped that she wasn't coming down with something. She had back to back interviews lined up all week, she couldn't afford to be getting ill now. "Do you work here?" Alice changed the subject, gesturing to Caleb's brown leather satchel.

"You could say that," Caleb answered cryptically. "I'm a messenger, I'm here to collect a package." They fell silent and Alice turned her attention to the numbers above the elevator doors. Fifth floor, fourth, third, second, first, and then finally, the ground floor.

Before the lift had come to a complete halt Caleb turned to Alice and smiled kindly. "You are my package Alice, I am the messenger for death, I have come to deliver you safely home." Alice looked slowly down at her pale blue interview outfit, a bloody stain across her heart, surprise registering across her face. "The bullet didn't just hit the man interviewing you Alice, it passed through you first." Caleb took her hand gently as the elevator doors opened and tugged her forwards. "Come, there are people waiting to see you."

THE WEDDING

As perfect as the ceremony had been, it was soon over, the balding minister proclaiming Gemma and Mike to be husband and wife. She had looked stunning in her white gown, but then she always looked stunning, the envious stares of her guests lingering on her as she moved around the room. Marrying Mike really had been a dream come true, nothing would ever come between them again, especially not her sister.

She knew that Mike had been surprised when Stella had sent her apologies to their wedding, they had always gotten along so well. She wasn't oblivious to the hushed whispers of some of her guests, disapproving of her sister's absence. She wisely held her tongue, her sister had been a thorn in her side her entire life, had even had the cheek to try and derail her wedding, coming to her the month before the wedding, confessing that she had fallen in love with Mike.

Stella had actually had the nerve to ask Gemma to break off her engagement so that she could be with Mike. No, she wasn't at all sorry that her sister had missed her big day. Actually, she had planned it that way, had faked a dream holiday competition for her sister to win, had been only too happy to share the news that her sister was enjoying her holiday so much that she had decided to extend it. She knew that her sister was drowning at home, had been under enormous stress helping their father to run the farm. She also knew that her sister was not planning on returning, had promised her that she would keep that fact a secret as she kissed her goodbye.

The wedding reception was flawless, the barn decked out in twinkling lights, their reflections dancing off the still water of the dam. This had been a perfect spot for the reception, she was glad she had brought her sister here the last time they had met, it was almost as if she was with them after all. Mike watched his wife quietly, standing on the balcony, away from the soft lights of the reception, she looked different, harsher somehow.

He drew her into his arms, his knuckles brushed a tendril of hair off her face, tucking it behind her ear, grazing softly across a raised scar. His fingers faltered, he knew his wife didn't have any scars, but her sister did. A single scar behind her ear, a childhood prank gone wrong.

"Gemma?" A frown marred his features at the silence, brows knitting together in confusion, eyes widening in horror as realisation dawned. "Stella?" His voice was barely a whisper, raspy, as if he had forgotten how to speak. His wife turned to face him, expression carefully calculated, a ghost of a smile gracing her face. "Cut!" The director's call broke the spell, applause breaking out as they wrapped on the final scene. There was an Oscar in this thriller, he just knew it!

THE CLAIRVOYANT

Aeryn shook her head in disbelief as she left the glare of the magic store behind her. Honestly, what a gimmick! She wondered how long the clairvoyant had worked there, he didn't seem terribly convincing, claiming her life was in danger from a mysterious stranger. Very unlikely! She paused to check the time of her phone, unaware of the figure slipping silently from the magic shop and falling into step behind her.

The theme park resembled a graveyard, deserted except for a few die-hard patrons, the usual hordes of boisterously loud families having been scared away by the never ceasing drizzling rain. Connor didn't mind, he preferred it this way, it was easier to watch her undetected, to follow slowly from a safe distance. Crowds just got in his way. His lopsided footsteps were muffed against the cobblestone path by the rain trickling off the sagging awnings above. She had no idea that she was being followed, Connor smirked to himself. She was just like all the others, oblivious until the end.

The winding path curved to follow the arc of the river slicing through the park, framed by bright hibiscus trees all in bloom. He watched her pause, as so many before her, at the wishing well bridge. The diluted sunlight shimmered across the lake below, briefly illuminating the crystal-clear surface, a mirror for her perfect reflection. She was breathtakingly beautiful. Copper hair fell in curls to frame her face, murky sea green eyes as deep as the ocean to guard her secrets. Out of everyone he had killed over the years, she was by far his prettiest victim.

He advanced silently, patting his jacket pocket, feeling reassurance that his taser was nice and close. His hand trembled as he reached out to touch her, her curls brushing his fingers as she turned, eyes wide. "You're the clairvoyant!" recognition flared in her eyes. "You're not very good," she smirked.

"I wouldn't be so sure," Connor advanced confidently, the ghost of a grin snaking across his face.

"I know what it is you do, I have seen you, watched you when you thought no one else was around," her statement brought him to a sudden stop, hand poised over his taser. She must be joking, talking about something else perhaps. There was no way that she could know, was there?

Connor looked at her closely. Where was her hair? Gone were the masses of curls, instead seaweed and algae tangled in a riot of knots around her garish face. Her mouth opened, and Connor's ears filled with a song so pure it made his heart ache. He felt like he was floating, or falling, her sinewed limbs tangled with his until there was nothing. Connor grew still, eyes empty, mouth contorted in a silent scream.

Aeryn released him slowly back to the surface of the lake, smiling as she watched him float above her like a human shaped balloon. He was just like all the others, oblivious until the end.

THE GRAVE

I ached to move. From my perch on the side of the service road I could see it was deserted, it would be hours before anyone came past, months perhaps, before my body would be discovered partially hidden amongst the tall grasses.

The faint scent of lemon wafted along the breeze, carried across the bay with the unfettered laughter of the café patrons. A night of celebration, fireworks exploded overhead, splash after splash of colour painting the inky night sky.

I never thought that I would end up here, I was always the safe one, I never took unnecessary risks. While my friends would stay out for hours on end, I always kept perfectly to my curfew. I watched as my friends journeyed the world chasing the thrill of another escapade, happily settling in bustling cities in exotic far flung places.

I had my own share of adventures, was lucky enough to explore many cultures and countries on Earth, yet my internal compass always steered me safely back home again. I was dependable, but never boring. I thought I was invincible, the naivety of the young.

I was in Europe when it happened, the war. All foreigners, even Australians, were suddenly feared, ostracised, banned. There was mass panic as the war spread across the globe, and fear controlled the population. Millions of people were displaced, desperate to make it home before it was too late. Country after country closed its borders, strangers were refused entry, those that were already there were shunned. The world fell into disarray. Stocks plummeted, bodies piled up, grocery items were stockpiled.

My government did everything they could to bring me home. Leaders met, relief packages were announced, humanitarian aid dispatched. As the crisis escalated, travel bans were lifted temporarily, and we were all rounded up and shipped home.

My relief at being on home soil was short lived. Worry was etched onto every face, our economy, once so strong, was crumbling. People were being labelled 'un-Australian', it was every man for himself, gone were the days of helping out your neighbour. People remained prisoners, too scared to venture from their homes.

My family business crumbled, and I was quite literally sold to the highest bidder. I was dragged out here onto the road and chained down. Starved of food and attention, my feet cracked and blistered, there are ribbons of rubber jutting out where my shoes once sat. The trademark ivory pigment I was once so proud of is discoloured and blotchy, my skin peeling off. I am hardly recognisable anymore, merely a shell of my former self.

Would you believe that I was famous once? Adored. People would gather, waiting, just to try to spot me. I had fan clubs, and millions of followers on social media. I was an icon. A proud airliner transporting scores of passengers throughout the skies. Skies that are clear now, silent. I sit here on the airport apron, derelict, rotted, forgotten.

This is my grave, and my legacy.

SECRETS

Five bodies, all with the same vacant look on their faces. Their mouths opened in a little O of surprise; eyes slightly wide. Mike shook his head. Poor bastards, they never saw it coming. He was surprised, to be honest. What did his family think he was doing up so late every night? A crossword puzzle?

The new clothes he had bought to blend in; the old mattress he had replaced with something state of the art, his back needing a good night sleep after the long hours he was putting in; the expensive coffee machine he claimed he had won, brewing only the best to keep him buzzing through the long nights. Yeesh! For a bunch of naughties or millennials or whatever they were supposed to be this decade, they sure had been slow. Were they not the least bit curious?

"I don't know what to say," it was his son, John, who found his voice first, no surprise to Mike. "Why didn't you tell us?" Yeah right, as if! Mike was an ex-police officer, he spent his entire life lying, trading in the subtle art of keeping secrets, from everyone, even his own family. He thought about some of the secrets that he had kept from them and shuddered. If only they knew.

The idea had come to him quite suddenly one uneventful morning, as he sat contemplating his breakfast, poached eggs on toast – again, wondering at the possibility of cutting his tongue off in an attempt to avoid his breakfast, far preferable than hurting his daughter in law's feelings, surely? This was what his life had become, this monotony.

He was bored stupid, and so his idea had started to form and take root in his mind. The more he thought about it, the more it made sense. After all, his wife was dead, and he was lonely, what did he have to lose? It had started out innocently enough, an email here and there, a quickie every month, just to keep his skills sharp.

Things quickly snowballed out of control, Mike was now fully invested, pounding away every night until dawn streaked across the sky and his family began to stir. He tried to convince himself it was his reward, the silver lining for getting old and being forced into retirement was that he now had time to pursue his passions, which, to his surprise, were netting him a small fortune.

The truth was far simpler, he enjoyed it. It was exhilarating, the back and forth, the suspense, the inevitable climax that left his heart racing. He could never have done this when his wife was alive, the risk was far too great, but now, what did he have to lose? The demand had surprised even Mike. Who knew that novels featuring a murderous vigilante copper could be so lucrative? He had promoted the series as fiction, after all, there was no need for his family to know all of his secrets.

Not just yet anyway.

THE COMPETITION

Just because people said that she was a cold-hearted ice queen, didn't make it true. On the contrary, Amanda had feelings. Well, she had little twinges, vestiges of feelings, buried deep down inside, but they were still there nonetheless. Take today for example, grand final day, her favourite day of the year, surpassing all holidays and mid-year sales. There were some critics who had said that today would never happen, given the season that they had endured, their most controversial one yet!

They had been plagued with injuries, people still spoke about their strongest competitor, impaled with a red-hot blade. He was out of the game naturally; after all, it is near impossible to perform successfully with only one eye! There had been other, less dramatic wounds too. A concussion from a fall, and a broken leg from a scrum, nothing too serious. There had been a bad omen right from the start, if you believed in those sorts of superstitions, which Amanda did not.

Still, it had been a huge disappointment when Timmy had missed the boat for their first away competition, the debacle had seen him out for the remainder of the season. Who knew if he would get another chance to play? That wasn't the only controversy, Amanda knew there had been subtle attempts at sabotage, the switched bottles here, the missing towel there. Not to mention the overt instances of blackmailing!

Amanda had her suspicions about who was behind it all, and she was on high alert for today, she intended to watch every little movement, to flush the perpetrator out once and for all. If there was one thing that Amanda hated, it was a cheater. The grand final started with a bang, literally as it happened, one of the floodlights exploding in a shower of tiny sparks. Not to be deterred, the competition raged on, just as fierce as it always is, everyone vying for one last chance to impress, never knowing just who would be watching.

The sound of the crowd gathered in the arena was deafening, the heat was almost unbearable, as tensions and egos ran high and tempers flared. Blood pounded in Amanda's ears as she watched with hawk like eyes, just waiting for someone to put a foot wrong. She thrived on this drama, the fierce battle to the end, the pinnacle of the season. She was in her element here, shouting out instructions and reminders, cursing and waving her fist in the air at those foolish enough to ignore her warnings.

Her husband Sam thought she was mad, screaming at the television set, but he had never understood her obsession with competition cooking shows, her insistence of watching them every single night. She had never missed an episode, not in eleven seasons, how could she? She was well and truly addicted. After all, no fictionalised drama any scriptwriter could invent would ever be able to top the real-life drama playing out in "Baking Jubilee".

PRISON

Alice froze. There it was again, that screaming! She looked around desperately, searching for the source, surely it had originated from nearby, a wounded animal perhaps? The sound was unlike any Alice had ever heard before, pure pain, it chilled her to her core. She had to find it, she had to help. She pressed on, unsure of her surrounds, stumbling over uneven ground, tree branches scratching at her face. A clearing opened up in front of her and she slowed, surprised to see a woman waiting for her, a break in the tree canopy bathing her in a golden light.

"I knew I would see you again," she embraced Alice, smiling warmly. "Come with me, I know you must have questions," her leathery hands linked with Alice's, leading her along a winding path.

"Who are you?" Alice was tired, and this stranger, who didn't feel like a stranger, was welcoming, comfort. Alice thought that this would be what Peace looked like, if Peace was a person.

"Trust yourself, you know who I am."

"I don't remember you," Alice mourned. She would have liked this stranger; of that she was sure, they would have been firm friends. The screaming grew louder, as Alice was led down a narrow stone staircase, spiralling around and around. Were they lost?

"Here we are," the stranger spoke, the staircase giving way to a sunken room containing a single table upon which sat a package, the glossy sheen of the waxed paper filling Alice with uncertainty.

"What is this place?" Alice jumped, her voice echoing strangely as the screaming stopped suddenly.

"You already know," the stranger moved around the room, humming softly.

"I don't."

"Don't worry, it will come to you later."

"How did I get here."

"We walked."

"No, to this place, the forest…" Alice trailed off. "All the screaming. Is this a prison?"

"A prison? In a way," the stranger nodded thoughtfully. "The guard is the one screaming, it is what traps you here, their pain, their past mistakes and lost dreams. It is the most powerful type of prison. You brought yourself here Alice, you always bring yourself."

"That doesn't make sense, I just woke up here. How do I get home?" Alice panicked.

"To leave here, the guard must be defeated. Once that happens, you will be free," the stranger explained slowly. "You have always known that."

"The guard?" Alice glances around the room dubiously. "What do they guard?"

"Everything that ever was and ever will be," the stranger answered cryptically.

"How do we defeat him? Will you help me?"
"There is only one person who can defeat the guard Alice."
"Who?"
"The guard."
"I don't understand."
"The only person who can defeat the guard is the guard, they have all the power, they control everything in this place. Don't you remember Alice? You already know all the answers to the questions you have asked; you know everything."

"Who is the guard?" Alice held her breath, fearing the answer.
"You are."

THE CLEANER

The brush glides across the canvas, flecks of grey mingling with stormy blue, creating the perfect shade. I chew on my bottom lip, analysing my progress critically. My entire being buzzes with anticipation, only a few more hours to go until he's finished, my portrait of Dennis Lynne.

I wasn't always an artist. I used to be a legal secretary, trading in shorthand and gossip equally, completely unaware of the talent I possessed.

I remember the exact moment that my life changed, a Wednesday, nondescript apart from the fact that I had an appointment downtown. Running late, the only spot I could find to park was outside a dirty looking laundromat.

I was about to step out of my car when I saw him, a face I would never forget, the face of the man who had cold bloodedly murdered my parents, leaving me an orphan at fourteen. If I had not spent the night at a friend's house, I would not be alive today. The courts had done their duty and convicted him, and I had been sent to live with my aunt and uncle, art collectors who loved and protected me fearlessly. The last any of us had heard was that John Michaels had been granted parole, given a fake identity, and relocated to a new suburb.

It was my aunt and uncle that I turned to, my anger boiling away, my breath coming in short gasps, fists clenched. I lurched around their lounge room, snatching up items and flinging them at the wall, revelling in the satisfying sounds of objects smashing on impact, until exhausted, I sank into their arms. It was my uncle who cleaned up, while my aunt gently led me through to her study, where she presented me with a box full of tiny tubes of paint. She encouraged me to pour all my feelings into a painting, assuring me that I would find it cathartic.

I painted John Michaels first, an overbright scene showing him sprawled in a dirty laundromat, blood oozing from a fatal stab wound to his neck. It was a relief to have him out of my head and onto the canvas. My relief turned to astonishment the following day, with the local newspaper reporting that John Michaels had been found dead in a local laundromat, with a fatal stab wound to his neck. The crime scene photograph they printed was identical to my painting.

My aunt had been right, I did find painting cathartic. Just as she was right when she said there would be a buyer, a niche market for my artistic manifestation talents. I have never been busier, and if asked, I smile and tell people that I am a cleaner.

I add the final touches to my portrait of Dennis Lynne, notorious human trafficker, his face contorted in fear, heavy dirt breaking through the lid of the crudely sealed coffin. I sign my painting as I always do, with the time it was finished.

THE LIBRARY

I smelt him before he came around the corner, nothing could mask the pungent odour of horses and sweat. He comes into my library at exactly twelve noon every day, this nameless cowboy with grubby hands. He sits in the same beige armchair, backpack at his feet, coffee in one hand, just watching her. At first, I was untouched by his daily routine, but the more he watched her, the more curious I became. You see, people watching is my little game, something to break up the monotony of my day.

It was during the second week of his visits that he noticed me sitting here. He paused at my table every day; fingers outstretched as if to touch me. She was furious when she saw him, sitting me at her desk, where he couldn't menace me. That didn't deter him, and as the days wore on, she became increasingly annoyed by his presence, going out of her way to avoid him.

Last night was the final time I saw the nameless man. She was working late, as she usually did, printing off overdue letters to be mailed out, when I heard the soft thud of a door closing. She turned, surprised to see him, ordering him out. He ignored her demands, stalking towards me, eyes glinting, grabbing me roughly. She snatched up the phone and threatened to call the police. He stilled, turning slowly, a smirk forming on his face. He looked at me for a moment before I was flung across the room, landing hard on the table, feeling something tear. I couldn't more, unable to help, forced to watch on helplessly as the nameless man grew menacingly closer to her, backing her into a corner, and with gloved hands wrapped tightly around her throat, drew the last remaining breath from her. He laughed as she crumpled to his feet, barely glancing in my direction as he pushed a heavy bookcase on top of her before casually walking out, smirking.

As daylight slowly began to creep into the room, Cupids library slowly filled up with police. The librarians broken body remained sprawled beneath an upturned bookcase, the tinned music from the overhead speakers startlingly out of place. I watch the detectives, mechanical in the way they operate, they train for this, but no one expected it to happen in their town. They spent hours searching for clues, exhausted every lead and investigated every angle, but I knew they would never find him. The nameless man was clever, he had become a regular fixture in my library, he was polite, and never raised suspicion. A small-town library, there were no security cameras, and no one came forward. There were no witnesses, well, unless you count me. You see, if the police knew to access the library records, they would see that the nameless man had tried to order me, had tried to pick me up last week, but was refused.

Rare books are not allowed to leave the library.

SEVEN DAYS

Her hand fumbles around on the bedside table until she finds what she is looking for, pressing the home button on her phone, she illuminates the screen. Urgh! It is already eleven o'clock, she was going to be late, again, no doubt delighting her perfectly punctual sister. Sighing deeply, she threw back the covers and swung her legs off the bed, rising and crossing the hall to the bathroom. Although she had a week off from work stretching out in front of her, she was already feeling exhausted, and lunch with her sister was just the start of her crazy busy week.

Jess hurried through her shower, pulling her mousy brown curly hair into a messy bun and donning a form fitting red dress with a slit that she knew would have her sister's eyebrows disappearing into her hair. Good, she smirked at the thought as she strutted down the street to the nearby Red Dog Café, her diamante covered stilettos sparkling in the sun, enjoying the stares she elicited from strangers passing her by. Her sister Carol was already at the café, her navy-blue cardigan and black shift dress as boring as her plain straight brown ponytail. Jess didn't need to look to know that underneath the table Carol would be wearing plain black ballet flats, the only shoes she ever wore.

"Jesus Christ!" Jess greeted her sister. "You look like you are sixty years old and going to a fucking funeral" she sneered, slumping into a chair opposite her and crossing her legs, the slit in her dress falling softly to reveal her hip bone.

"Jess!" Carol hissed, looking around frantically. "Language" she admonished. Lips pressed firmly together, Carol watched as Jess picked up a menu, determined that she would not mention her dress. Carol knew that Jess only wore outfits like this to annoy her, and while they didn't exactly move in the same circles socially, Carol was sure that Jess had more conservative clothes. At least, she really hoped that she did.

Lunch was strained, as it usually was. Although they were sisters, and had once been quite close, Carol and Jess no longer had anything in common. Carol had been a single teenage mum and had spent years working in admin to provide for her son. Two years ago, she had met and married Matthew, a local doctor, and she had resigned from her job. Blissfully happy, Carol now spent her days caring for her family, running their house and volunteering for causes that she was passionate about. Jess on the other hand had attended university, graduating with a degree in law and an over inflated sense of entitlement.

Every time the sisters spoke, Jess had a new job, a new boyfriend, and more drama than NIDA. Today was no different, with Jess informing Carol that she had quite her latest job after only three months, which was not her fault, naturally someone else was to blame. Someone else was always to blame. Carol found herself wishing that she had an excuse to leave early, she found Jess's repetitive dialogue exhausting to sit through, and tried not to look relieved when the waiter brought the bill over. Carol paid without hesitation, ignoring the niggling feeling of guilt nipping at her subconscious. This wasn't a duty lunch, she reminded herself sternly, she loved her sister, she really did, she wasn't going to lose touch with her just because they had nothing in common.

Saying goodbye, Carol watched Jess float down the street as if she didn't have a care in the world. Jess looked vibrant and self-confident, but something was niggling at Carol. With a shrug she crossed the street to her car, she would ask Jess about it when they had lunch together next month.

Jess was already smiling when she woke the following day. Last night she had called her best friend Joanne and convinced her to call in sick to work today so that the two of them could travel into the city to go shopping. Jess adored shopping, and knew that no matter how you were feeling, everything could be fixed with a new purchase. The moment that the shop assistant handed over a crisp new bag, heavy with the weight of the item inside, was pure ecstasy. Better than any drugs Jess had ever tried, and she had tried almost everything that was available. Just last night her married neighbours had mixed her a special blend of ice laced weed, with a few extra ingredients thrown in to make it truly memorable. Jess's Special Sauce they had called it as they had shared it, and her, well into the early hours of the morning.

Meeting at the local train station, Joanne greets Jess with a lingering kiss, her hand sliding down to cup Jess's bottom, pressing her closer, leaving both girls breathless.

Although neither Jess nor Joanne identified as being gay, they loved sex, and sex with each other, as they discovered one drunken night, was hard and hot, leaving both girls completely spent, with an unquenchable thirst for each other that they had yet to quell.

The shopping mall was busy, just the way Jess liked it. Everywhere you looked there were people making purchases, carrying pretty boxes and bags around, blissful looks on their faces. Smiling, Jess grabbed Joanne's hand, pulling her into a dress shop, reverently fingering the silky fabrics, letting them slowly slide through her fingers. At Joanne's urging Jess tried on a couple of short party dresses, treating her to an impromptu Pretty Woman inspired fashion show before deciding to buy both of them. That was the best thing about Joanne, Jess thought, she was always happy to encourage Jess to buy whatever it was that she wanted. After all, it was only money, she could always make more if she needed to.

Several hours later, hundreds of dollars' worth
of bags piled around them, Joanne and Jess
finally stopped for lunch, deciding on a
seafood restaurant. Jess didn't exactly like
seafood, but they served the best wine labels
at this restaurant, and Jess loved her alcohol.
Reenergised from lobster and champagne, and
keen to return to their shopping spree, Jess
and Joanne breezed out of the restaurant as if
they owned the place, dissolving into fits of
laughter as they turned the corner out of sight
and realised that neither of them had
remembered to pay the bill sitting discreetly
on the table. Oh well, Jess reasoned, it wasn't
as if the restaurant couldn't afford it, they
were a premier establishment after all, the
owners were obviously loaded.

Still basking in their good fortune, Jess and
Joanne headed for the make-up section of a
major department store, Jess needed to
replace her Twisted Sister Poison Purple
glitter eye shadow before she went clubbing
on Saturday. Which is how she found herself,

an hour later, sitting in the security office of the shopping mall, an innocent smirk of disbelief gracing her face. Seriously, she was a lawyer for heaven's sake, not some petty criminal, of course she intended to purchase the eyeshadow, it had obviously mistakenly fallen into one of her other shopping bags when she had tossed it towards the shopping basket she was using, that was all. The store manager didn't believe her, and security had issued her with a three month ban of the shopping mall. Worse of all, the store had refused to allow her to purchase the eyeshadow, and now she would need to use something else on Saturday.

After the debacle of Tuesday, Jess felt particularly irritated, and had spent nearly all day on Wednesday online, leaving nasty customer reviews for all of the stores she had patronised the day before. If they thought for one second that they could ban her from shopping there without any retribution, they were sorely mistaken. Jess slept soundly that night, thanks to the migraine tablets she had washed down with a bottle of wine, or was it two? With all of her friends at work, Jess spent Thursday at home, half-heartedly doing housework and paying a stack of bills that had been sitting, neglected, on the kitchen counter for several weeks.

Jess hated having to adult, as she called it, and by the end of Thursday had tired of being responsible. After posting a selfie of her pouty face to social media, she sat back and waited for the invitations to roll in. One thing Jess never lacked was invitations, and sure enough, within minutes of her photo being uploaded she had already received over a dozen invites, including one to attend a fashion show, which, although tempting, Jess declined. There had been a rather awkward incident at the last event the venue had hosted, and she wasn't entirely sure that her name had been removed from the venue's black list yet. She poured another glass of wine and flipped through the rest of her messages. Scott was in town, Jess smiled, he was always fun to be with, and always ready to party. She sent off a quick text message, and a spa day was arranged for the following day.

Peeking through her eyelashes over at Scott, their faces wrapped in heated plush white towels, Jess thought that this was the perfect way to spend a Friday. Jess adored Scott. Friends since university, Scott was a dedicated commercial pilot, happily married to James. It was actually James who had sent them both off for a massage, declaring that Scott and Jess had gone too long without a spa day. He was right of course, as he usually was.

The spa at Mombassa was divine, a favourite with Jess, not only for the treatments they supplied, but also for their location overlooking a secluded beach. Wrapped in the spa supplied robes, Jess and Scott lunched on the beach, catching up with each other's gossip and playing their favourite game of guessing the flaws and back stories of strangers passing by, the most outrageous, the better. Their day ended far too quickly for Jess's liking, and Scott drove her back home, promising not to let it be so long before their next spa day.

Jess woke late on Saturday afternoon, already anticipating her evening ahead. Saturday's were for partying and clubbing, and, if you were Jess, wild, uninhibited sex. Saturday's made the rest of the week bearable and gave Jess a reason to work so hard at the gym each lunch break. Jess had a light snack and spent the rest of the afternoon getting ready, paying particular attention to her eye makeup, hoping to try a new smoky eyed look she had seen online and instantly coveted. She knew it would look amazing on her flawless complexion, and it would have the added benefit of making her friends envious. Jess took great pride in looking good, in portraying a polished image to the world, whatever it cost her in time, effort or money, she knew that it was certainly worth it.

Jess adored The Vibe nightclub, it was the perfect destination for sweaty dancing and casual hook ups on a Saturday night. The fact that it was literally underground and catered to new and undiscovered heavy metal bands only added to the appeal. Walking into The Vibe, Jess spied her friends through the crowd and made her way slowly across the crowded dance floor, her incredibly mini silver sequin dress sparkling under the lights, catching the eyes of several young men. Jess knew that at least one of them would approach her before the end of the night, the thought pleasing her. Jess never wanted for male company, or female company for that matter, and if none of her fellow clubbers appealed to her, Jess had a long list of friends with benefits, or fuck buddies as she called them, that she could hook up with at a moment's notice.

It didn't take long for someone to approach Jess, and introduce himself as Sam, a man she estimated to be in his late twenties, slim with well defined muscles. He looked as if he had stamina, which was always a turn on for Jess. She agreed to a dance, "Devil's Face" by The Regular Johns was playing, a dirty, grungy, slow song perfect for grinding in the dark with a perfect stranger. As the song neared its end, Jess leant up and whispered in Sam's ear, "Are you going to fuck with me Sam?" Her answer was his slow, sexy smile before his mouth came crashing down on hers, his tongue fighting hers for dominance, sucking and nipping, relishing in tasting her, drinking her in. Jess lifted a hand from the back of Sam's head and waved goodbye to her friends, she knew she wouldn't be seeing them again tonight.

Brunch, as far as Jess was concerned, happened far too early in the day. Seriously, what was wrong with lunch, or even dinner? Why did Sunday always need to mean a brunch with her friends? To be fair, it was a recovery brunch, which after last night, Jess sorely needed. Sam had, as she had suspected, stamina in spades, and Jess had more fun last night, for longer and in more positions, than she had been having in a long time. Her body ached in all the most delicious of places, and she knew it would be a long time before her body lost the imprint of Sam's touch.

Brunch was a subdued affair, everyone in her group sporting dark sunglasses and bright lipstick, as if that could somehow magically improve their washed out, pale complexions, and remove the scarlet stain of alcohol and sex inked across their psyches. They spoke of banal, normal topics, of workplace dramas and grocery specials, the type of conversations that Jess detested. She had begun to think that she should just stop coming to their regular Sunday brunch catch ups all together, she never got anything out of them, and always went away feeling rather repressed and needing a handful of pills and a large drink. Maybe she was feeling this way as she had to return to work tomorrow, pretend to be normal again after her week on holiday.

Yes, Jess decided, as she made her way home later that afternoon, she was sure that her return to work was the issue, the reason she suddenly felt so unhappy, so down. She almost felt normal, which, for Jess, was a horrifying thought. Is this how her sister felt day after day? A suffocating normalcy? Maybe she would feel better if she changed jobs? After all, the law firm she was working at was hardly well known or even especially busy, and Jess was bored. She needed excitement. Yes, a new job would help, she would start looking as soon as she got home, with a bit of luck she would find something almost immediately and would able to give her notice at work this week.

The group of young medical doctors moved in a huddle, rather like a swarm of bees or a flock of birds, when one veered, they all veered, when one stopped, they all stopped. It was rather fascinating to watch, like seeing a hospital ballet performance. All new to the hospital, the group of doctors, sixteen in all, were currently doing a three-month rotation in each of the main wards, including surgical, medical and psychiatry, after which they would be able to choose their field to specialise in. It was psychiatry that they were rotating through today, a walk through to familiarise themselves with the layout of the ward, and to introduce themselves to the current patients on the ward, to read through their case notes and answer any questions that they may have about having junior doctors shadow their usual caregiver.

It was their first patient that was of the most interest to the junior doctors, an actual case of Dissociative Identity Disorder, previously known as Multiple Personality Disorder. Incredibly rare, this patient was said to have at least five distinct personalities, and possibly even more. Following the registered psychiatrist into the room, unsure of what they were about to encounter, the junior doctors were surprised to be greeted by a plain white hospital room, empty except for a single bed against the wall, a pretty, middle

aged woman sitting on the edge, legs dangling over the side, was waiting for them.
"Hello Jess, these are the doctor's I was telling you about."

***

FLING WITH THE FLYING DOCTOR

A cynical doctor. A nurse with a secret. How far would you go for the person you loved?

Jurgen Cristo loves his role as a doctor working with the Royal Flying Doctor Service. Based in the isolated outback town of Alice Springs, his job is demanding, every call is another fight to save the life of a stranger. Betrayed by his ex-fiancé, he is cynical of relationships, vowing to never risk his heart again.

Meghan Richards is a compassionate and talented nurse working on the children's ward. Trapped by her past mistakes, she harbors a secret which has condemned her to a lifetime of singledom.

Jurgen and Meghan begin a casual romance, ultimately leading them to question everything they thought they wanted. When Jurgen's old flame appears, and Meghan's devastating secret is revealed, he makes the ultimate declaration to win back the woman he loves.

"Fling With The Flying Doctor" is a contemporary story of romance, recovery, and revelation, set in the harsh Australian desert, featuring strong main characters that are relatable and recognizable to modern day women.

ABOUT THE AUTHOR

Kathleen is a proud mother and foster mother.

She has also been, among other things, a circus performer, photographer, cake artist, tour guide, and wedding and event planner.

Her goals in life are simply to finish raising happy, imaginative, and inquisitive children; to make a real and tangible difference in the lives of others; and to keep writing novels for as long as she possibly can.

Kathleen makes her home in the isolated desert, surrounded by red dirt, striking mountain ranges, and endless clear blue skies. It is this stunning landscape that features as backdrop for many of her novels.

When she is not writing, you can find Kathleen hanging out with her boys, reading, or planning her next adventure!

CONNECT WITH KATHLEEN

Kathleen is active across the following social media platforms:

Website: www.kathleenryder.com
Instagram: @kathleenryderauthor
Twitter: @Kathleen__Ryder
Facebook: kathleenryderauthor
Pinterest: kathleenryderauthor